PAJAMAS

by **Livingston** and **Maggie Taylor**

illustrated by **Tim Bowers**

HBJ

GULLIVER BOOKS

HARCOURT BRACE JOVANOVICH

San Diego   Austin   Orlando

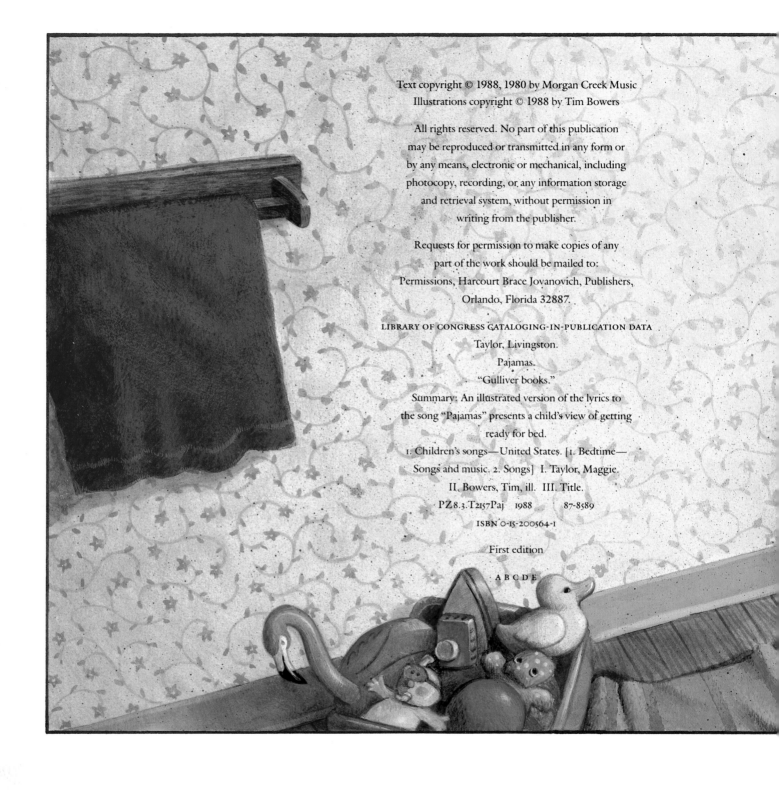

LIBRARY OF CONGRESS CATALOGING-IN-PUBLICATION DATA
Taylor, Livingston.
Pajamas.
"Gulliver books."
Summary: An illustrated version of the lyrics to
the song "Pajamas" presents a child's view of getting
ready for bed.
1. Children's songs—United States. [1. Bedtime—
Songs and music. 2. Songs] I. Taylor, Maggie.
II. Bowers, Tim, ill. III. Title.
PZ8.3.T2157Paj 1988 87-8589
ISBN 0-15-200564-1

First edition

A B C D E

To Mom and Dad
—T.B.

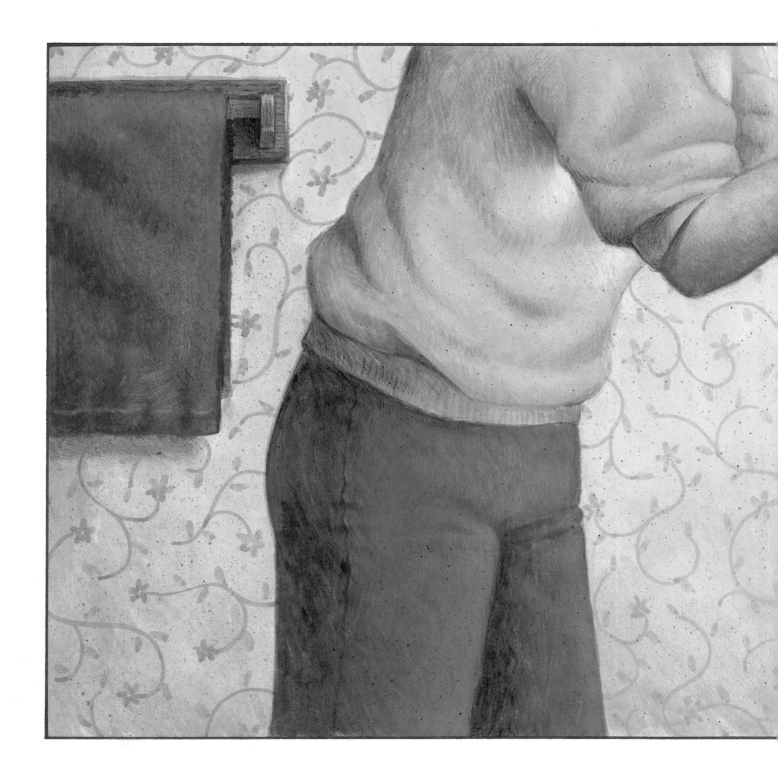

Mommy said, "Put them on."
I said, "No."

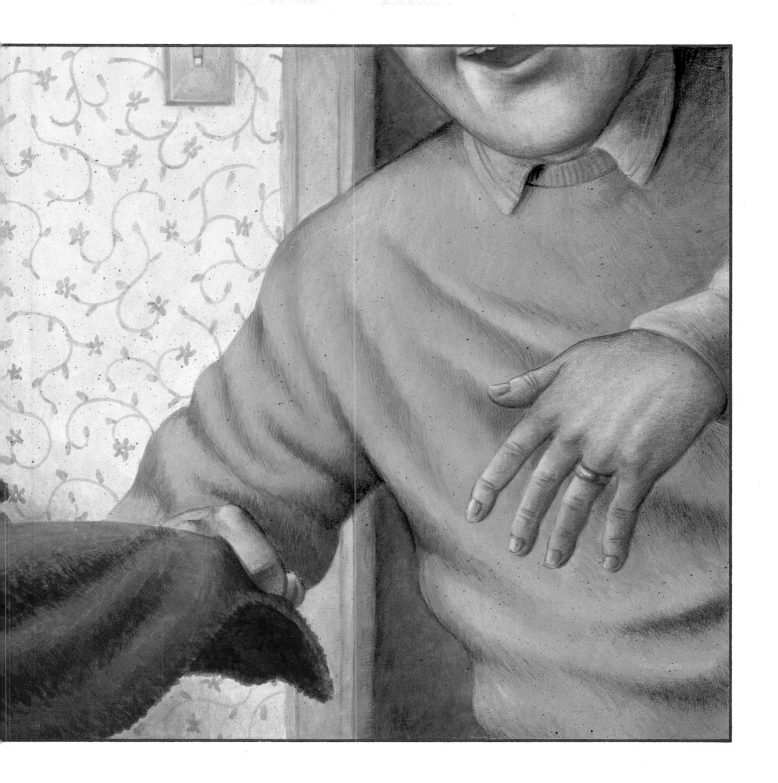

Daddy said, "Let's go."
So I said, "All right."

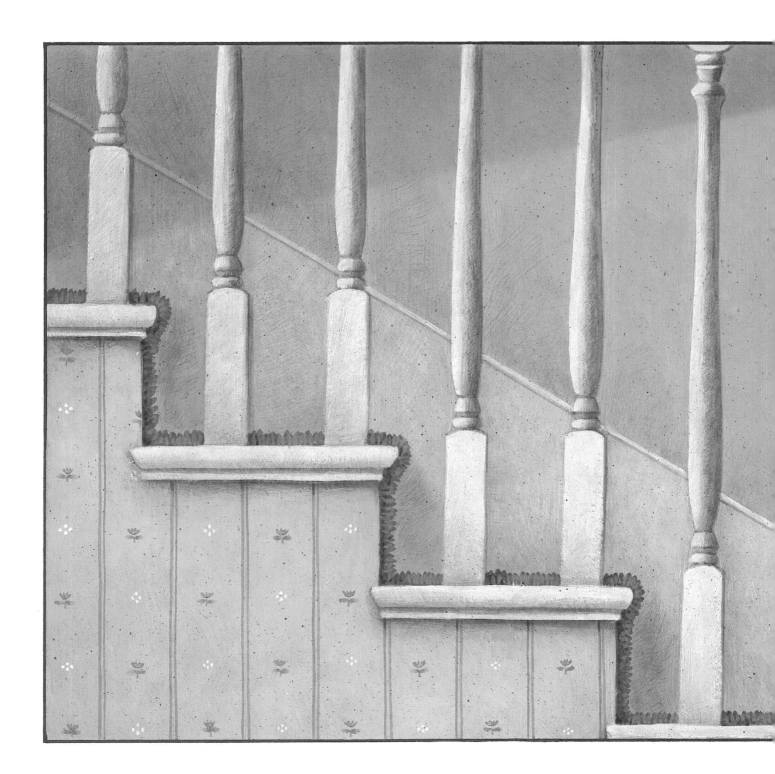

I'm clean, and I'm warm, and I'm out of sight!

I've got my pajamas on.

Before I go to bed I'm going to run around.

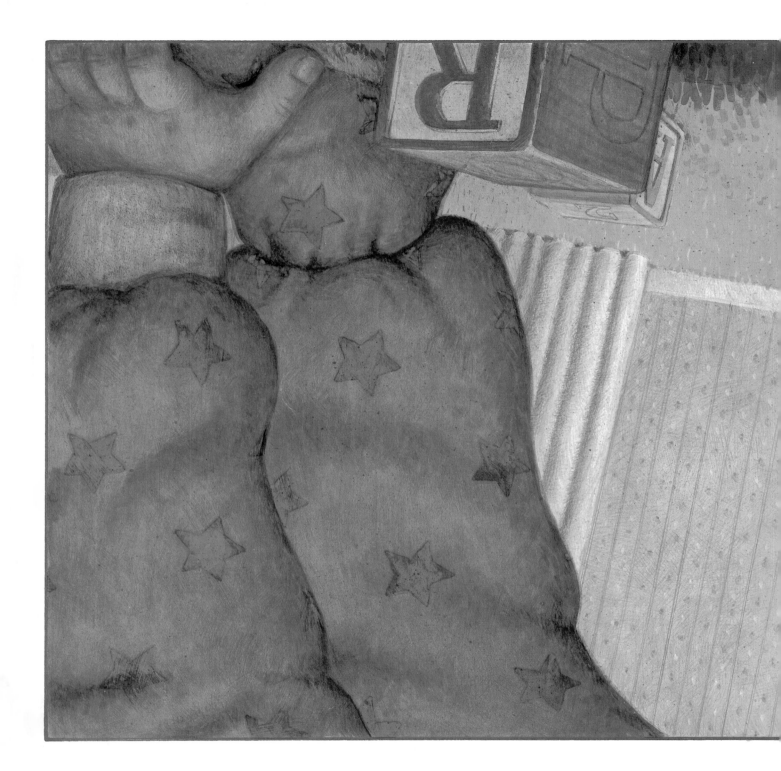

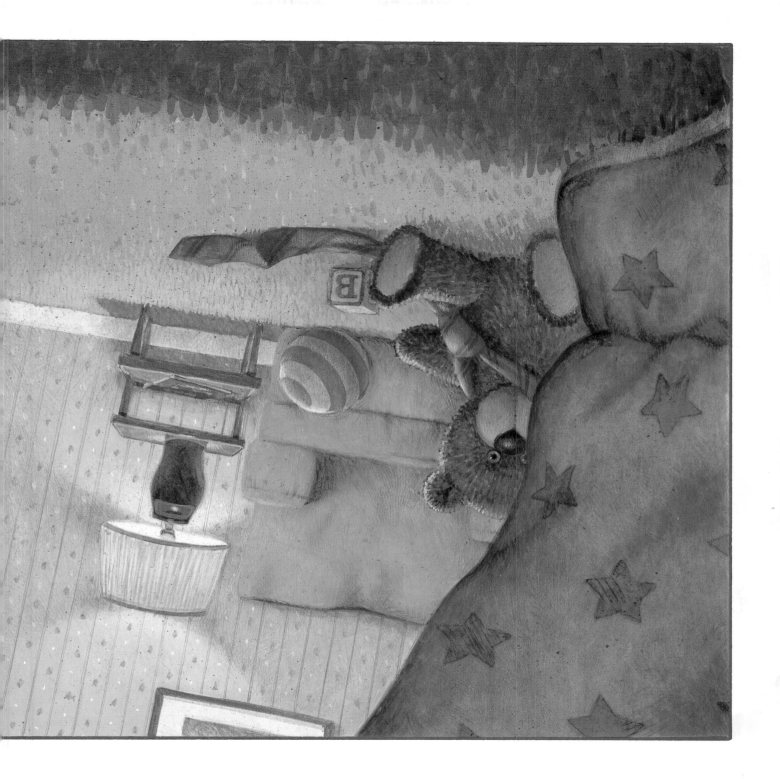

I'm standing on my head
and the world is upside down.

Me and Wilson, my teddy bear,
are going to do a lot of wiggling
before we go upstairs.

Watch out you lions, you tigers, you bears!

I've got my pajamas on.

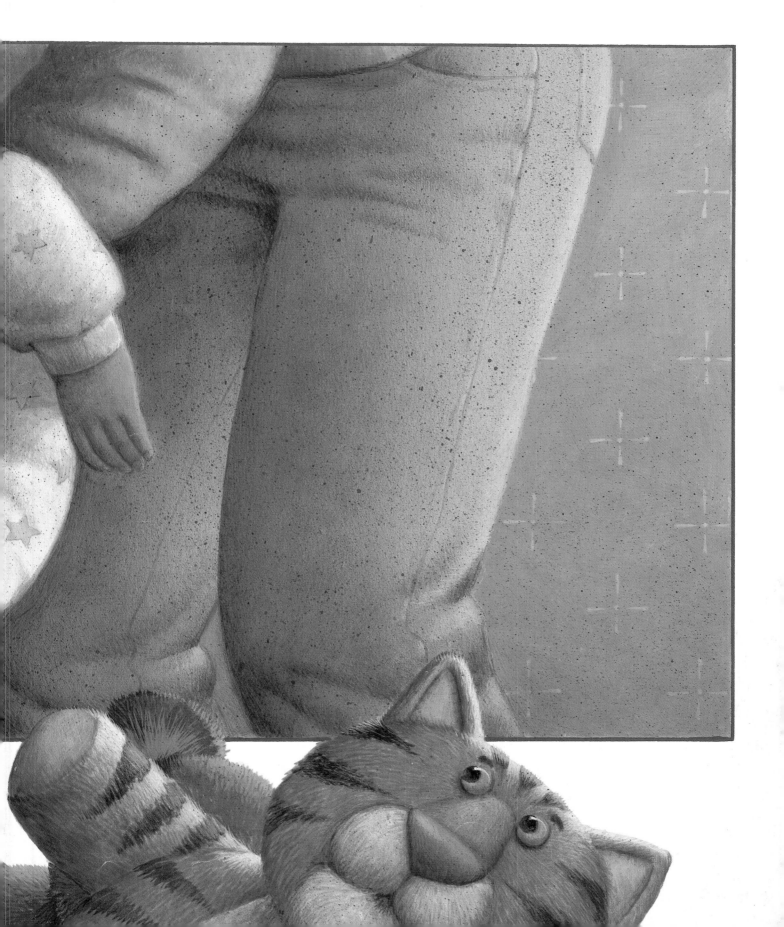

Now I'm in Daddy's lap, fading fast.

Wilson, if you want to mess around,
you'll have to do it alone.

I love being little, and I'll love being grown.

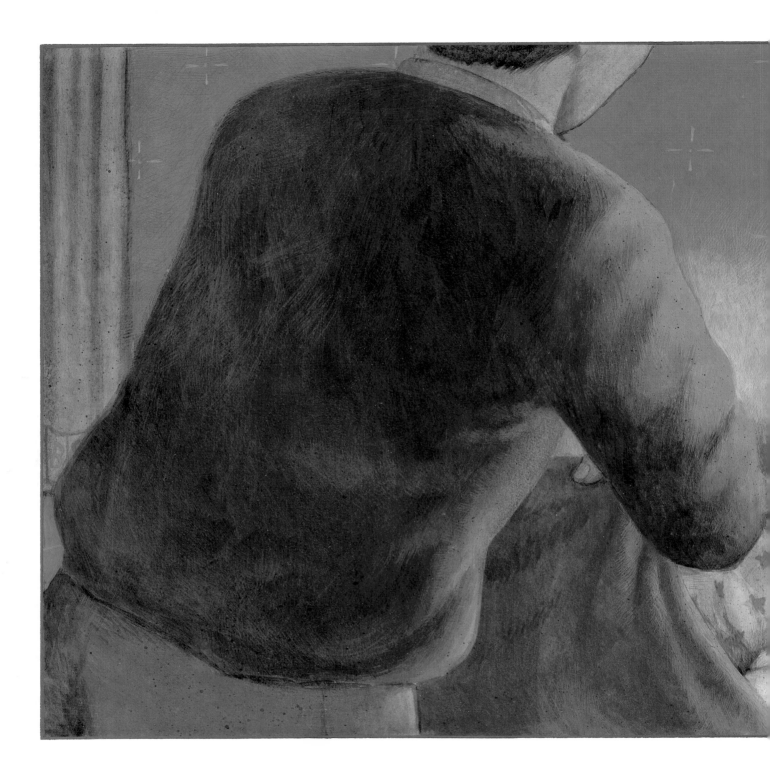

I've got my pajamas on.

The illustrations in this book were done in acrylic on 3-ply Strathmore paper.

The text type was set in Galliard by Thompson Type, San Diego, California.

Printed and bound by Tien Wah Press, Singapore

Production supervision by Warren Wallerstein

and Ginger Boyer

Designed by Nancy J. Ponichtera